To my father, "Bernie"

Copyright © 1994 by Ron Cohen

All rights reserved. No part of this book may be reproduced or utilized in any form
or by any means, electronic or mechanical, including photocopyng and recording,
or by any information storage and retrieval system, without permission in writing from
the Publisher. Inquiries should be addressed to Lothrop, Lee & Shepard Books,
a division of William Morrow & Company, Inc., 1350 Avenue of the Americas,
New York, New York 10019.   Printed in Singapore.

First Edition   1 2 3 4 5 6 7 8 9 10

Library of Congress Cataloging in Publication Data
Cohen, Ron. The ball / by Ron Cohen.
p.   cm. Summary: A father tells his son about going to his first baseball game
and getting a ball signed by Yogi Berra. ISBN 0-688-12390-2.— ISBN 0-688-12391-0
(lib. bdg.) — [1. Baseball—Fiction. 2. Fathers and sons — Fiction. 3. New York
(N.Y.) — Fiction.] I. Title. PZ7.C664Bal 1994 [E] — dc20   93-22938 CIP AC

Ron Cohen

My Dad's Baseball

Lothrop, Lee & Shepard Books   New York

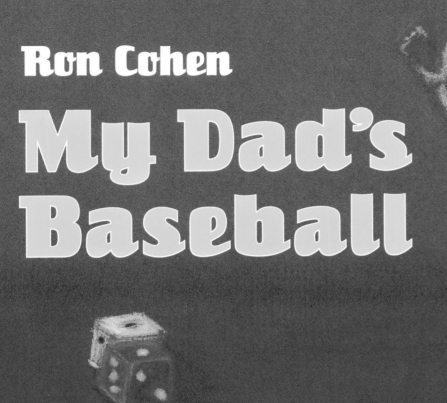

MY GRANDMA'S ATTIC IS BIG, and every inch of it is stuffed with memories. One day while I was helping my father move some old chairs up to the attic, I accidentally knocked over a box. Everything inside it tumbled to the floor.

"My ball!" my father shouted in surprise. He bent down and picked up an old yellowed baseball. Then he sat down next to me on the floor and leaned against some boxes.

"What's so special about it?" I asked.

This is the story he told me.

◆

Some days stay in your mind forever, Max. June 4, 1955, is one of them. I was seven years old, just your age.

My brother, your uncle Richard, woke me up that morning. "Today's the day," he said.

That afternoon Dad was taking Richard and me to our first baseball game—the New York Yankees versus the Detroit Tigers.

Almost everyone I knew hated the Yankees. Except Aunt Ethel—she loved them. She knew the averages and statistics of every single Yankee, and she seemed to know what they did at home, too. "Rizzuto got three hits today," she'd say."He must be eating a lot of fruit." Or "Mantle made a great catch. He probably went to bed before nine-thirty."

Dad and Richard rooted for the New York Giants. Richard loved their center fielder, Willie Mays. He was always trying to walk and talk like Willie—without much success. But he did a perfect imitation of Willie's basket catch. He practiced it everywhere: on his way to school, watching television, even during dinner. He'd toss the ball up and get under it, then *plop*— right into the old basket. Of course, Mom and Dad put their foot down on some occasions, like Uncle Lenny's wedding, and made him leave his ball and glove at home.

I was a Milwaukee Braves fan. Eddie Mathews was the Braves' third baseman, a great home-run hitter, and I loved him. I always had my Eddie Mathews baseball card with me. I stared at it a lot, and when I stared long enough, Eddie would talk to me. "Don't swing so hard," he'd tell me. "Keep your eyes on the ball. Try harder."

Aunt Ethel was always trying to turn me into a Yankees fan. "How can you root for a team that's nine hundred miles away when you have a great one four miles from your front door?" she'd say. But I loved the Braves from the moment I first saw their uniforms: the Indian on the sleeve, the tomahawk, the strong black and red against the bright white fabric. They were my team.

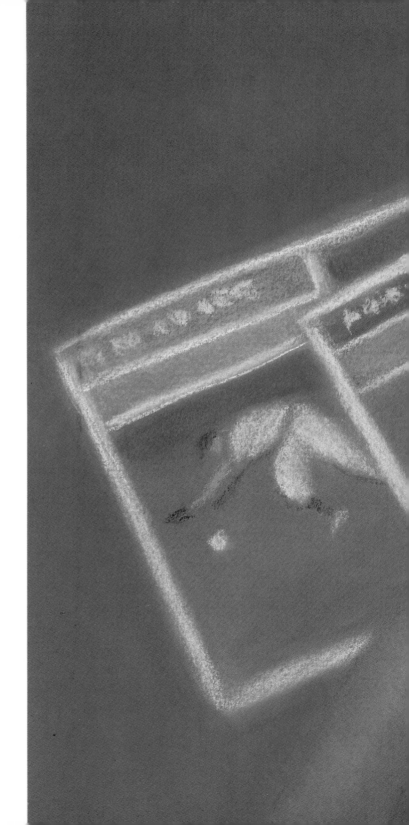

ED MATHEWS

Edwin Mathews

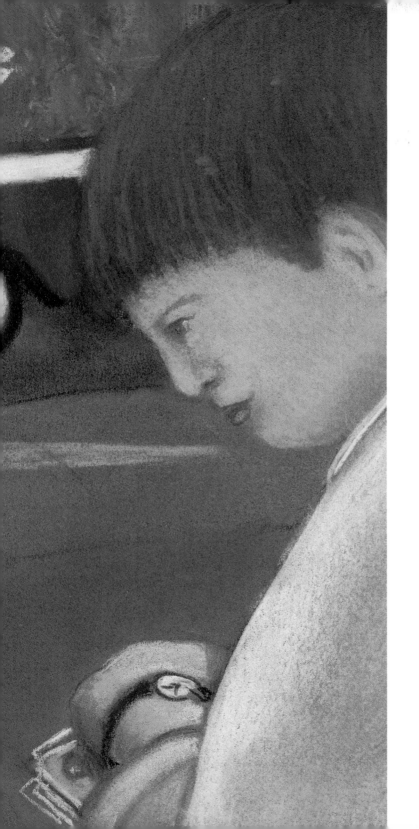

Even though the Braves weren't playing, I could hardly wait to get to the ball game that day. The morning crawled by. Richard and I sat on the stoop in front of our building. We pulled out all our Yankees and Tigers cards and piled them into two neat stacks. We read all the statistics, stacked the cards again, then played catch. I kept checking Richard's watch.

Finally Uncle Lenny drove up in his brand-new 1955 red-and-white Dodge. "I don't think Uncle Lenny's been out of that car since he got it," Richard whispered. "Every day he wants to drive us somewhere or just take us for a ride."

"Dad, hurry up. Uncle Lenny's here!" Richard yelled up at the window as we ran to the car and scrambled into the back.

"I hope your hands are clean," Uncle Lenny grumbled.

As soon as Dad got in beside him, we took off.

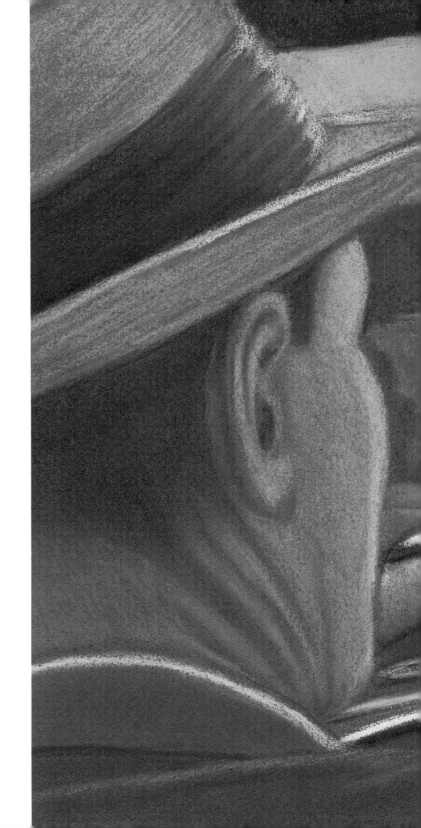

"So, it's Yankee Stadium today...your first baseball game...," said Uncle Lenny. "What are the gloves for? You kids aren't going to try and catch the ball if it's hit to you, are you? That would be a big mistake. We don't want any broken fingers or cracked heads. A baseball is hard ...and it's hit by very big men." He looked at us in the rearview mirror. "If that ball comes your way," he went on, "my advice to both of you is to hide. That's right, get down under your seats and hide!"

He and Dad argued, about stop signs and red lights and which way to turn, the rest of the way to the stadium. The drive took forever.

Finally, Uncle Lenny pulled up in front of the stadium and let us out. "I'll pick you up right here after the game. And remember what I told you," he called.

As we disappeared into the crowd, I could hear him shouting: "HIDE!"

Dad guided us through the gate and the crowd. "I'm going to take you to the very top of the stadium," he told us.

We walked up ramp after ramp, higher and higher, till finally, Yankee Stadium stretched itself out below me like some magical island surrounded by thousands of seats. Towering high above the seats was a huge greenish castle. I never saw grass so green or dirt so orange. The players looked even smaller than they did on our nine-inch television screen, and the spectators bobbed around like thousands of tiny dots.

As I stared out into all that space, I felt as if I was floating through a dream world. The size, the colors and sounds, made me dizzy.

Dad put his hand on my shoulder and shook me. "Let's go to our seats," he said.

We headed down to the lower right-field stands. "What are you going to do if the ball is hit to us?" I asked Richard. He looked at me and smiled. "I'll basket catch that sucker, that's what!" He pounded his glove and did a fake Willie Mays catch.

There was one Yankee player I sort of liked, Mickey Mantle. Aunt Ethel said he was going to be one of the greatest players ever. As the Yankees took the field, I put Dad's binoculars to my eyes and took a good look at Mickey in center field. He was chewing gum and blowing huge bubbles. That made me like him more—I liked bubble gum, too.

◆

When Mickey came up to bat, I asked Dad if we could move closer to home plate. I took his binoculars and watched Mickey bat. I recorded every detail: how he held the bat, stepped into the pitch, watched the ball, and finally shifted all his weight into one powerful fluid swing.

As the innings went by, the crowd got louder and louder. People yelled their advice to the players, they booed the umpires, they argued with each other about who the best players were. I just watched...and wondered what it felt like to be out on the field.

In the bottom of the sixth inning, the Yankees were behind four to two. Yogi Berra stepped to the plate with a man on first and two out. The pitcher wound up, and then Yogi swung. I heard the crack of the bat. The stadium turned strangely quiet as the ball went soaring.

Richard started pounding his glove. Suddenly, people were standing and shouting all around me. "It's coming this way!" someone yelled. Everyone was reaching and pushing and shouting. My heart was pounding. Uncle Lenny's voice was loud in my head: "HIDE!"

I dropped to my knees. When I looked up, the ball was sailing over everyone's outstretched hands. I heard it crash behind me. All around me people were jumping over seats, diving for the ball. I scooted under my seat.

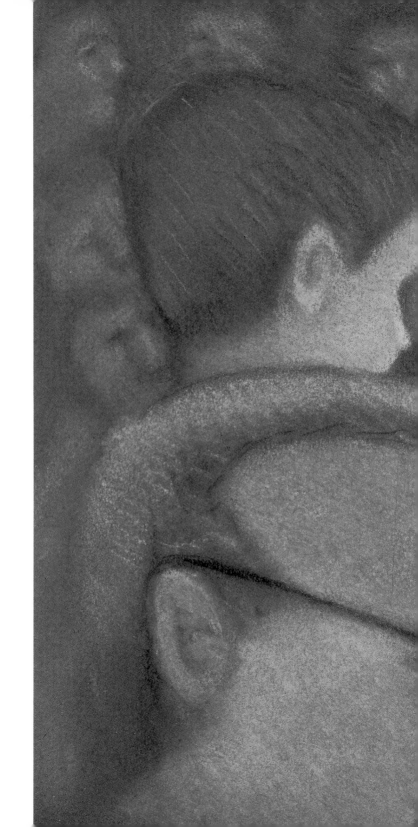

Hundreds of hands were frantically grabbing for the ball, and everyone around me was yelling. I slid as far back as I could.

Suddenly there it was, right in front of me. I reached out and grabbed the ball.

"I've got it!" I screamed. I jumped to my feet and held the ball high over my head. I handed it to Richard. Lots of people wanted to see it, so we passed it around. A kid behind me griped that he'd had it in his hand and should have gotten it. An old man said, "I've been going to baseball games for thirty years, and I've never gotten a ball."

I hardly saw the rest of the game. It all went by in a blur, as if I were dreaming. I kept waiting for someone to wake me up, but it was real, all of it. I was holding the ball that proved it.

Dad had to work the next day, but he arranged for Yogi to sign the ball for me. Uncle Lenny drove Richard and me to the stadium again.

"I want to give you some advice," Uncle Lenny said as we pulled up in the parking lot. "When in Rome, do as the Romans do."

I looked at Richard, wondering what Rome had to do with Yankee Stadium. Richard shrugged.

"That means, you get rid of that freakin' Braves cap," Uncle Lenny explained. "For the next twenty minutes, you're both going to be Yankee fans. When you pass through that door, you're in Rome."

I stuffed the cap into my pocket.

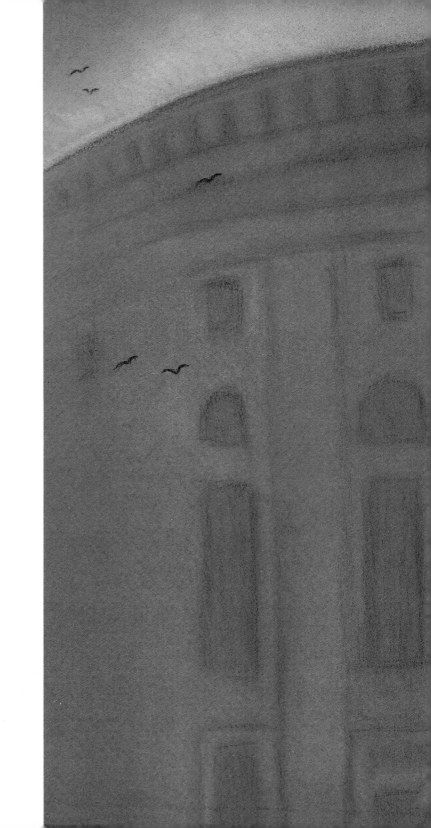

We entered a door marked PLAYERS ONLY. Inside, sitting on a bench right in front of me, was Yogi Berra.

"Which one of you kids caught the ball?" he asked.

"I did." I stepped forward.

"What's your name, kid?" Yogi asked.

"Ron, uh, Cohen," I told him.

"Well, Ron, what team do you root for?"

I swallowed hard. My hands began to sweat. I kept thinking about Rome and Romans and all that. But I couldn't say I was a Yankee fan no matter how hard I tried. I couldn't even get the word *Yankee* out of my mouth.

"Well?" said Yogi.

I had to say something. "I...I really...don't have a favorite team," I finally mumbled. "I just ...root...for individual players."

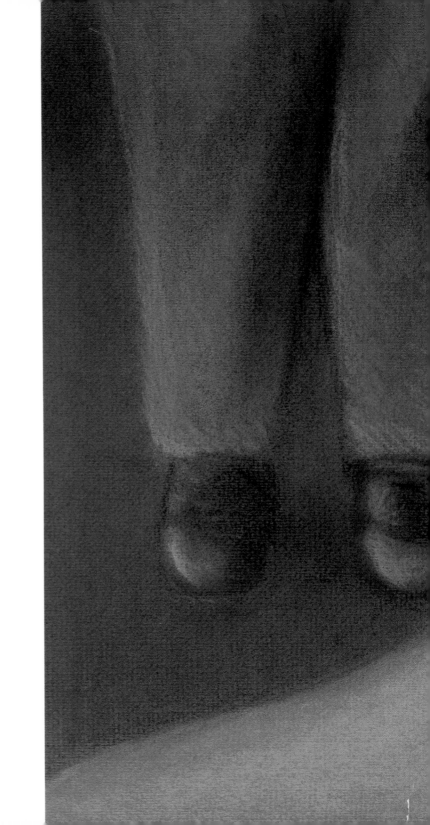

It didn't look like Yogi had heard me, and I was praying he wouldn't ask me to repeat what I'd said. He cocked his head and raised his eyebrows a little.

"Okay, let's see the ball," he said.

I reached into my pocket. As I pulled the ball out, my Braves cap fell to the floor. Everyone stared at it.

"Oh, you mean you're a *Braves* fan," said Yogi.

Then Yogi Berra put his hand on my shoulder and laughed.

"Let me tell you something, Ron," he said as he looked into my eyes. "You should always be who you are."

He signed the ball and stood up. "Who knows," he said. "I could be playing for the Braves one day."

Yogi handed me the ball. He smiled as we shook hands.

"That's the story," Dad said. "Yogi's signature is still sharp and clear, even after...thirty-seven years. I kept the ball in a box under my bed for years. Grandpa and Grandma moved, the ball got packed away, and I could never find it again. When you were born I searched everywhere for it. I wanted you to have it." Dad put his arm around me and placed the ball in my hand. "Now that you found it, I can finally give it to you."

I lay in bed that night, squeezing the ball tight, bits of my father's story swirling in my head as I fell asleep.